MICHAEL DAHL PRESENTS

SUPER FUNNY

JOKE BOOKS

# Screaming

## with

# Laughter

JOKES ABOUT GHOSTS, GHOULS,
ZOMBIES, DINOSAURS, BUGS,
AND OTHER SCARY CREATURES

PICTURE WINDOW BOOKS
a capstone imprint

## MICHAEL DAHL PRESENTS SUPER FUNNY JOKE BOOKS

are published by Picture Window Books
a Capstone Imprint
151 Good Counsel Drive, P.O. Box 669
Mankato, Minnesota 56002
www.capstonepub.com

*Dino Rib Ticklers* and *Monster Laughs* were previously published
by Picture Window Books © 2003
*Beastly Laughs*, *Creepy Crawlers*, and *Spooky Sillies*
were previously published by Picture Window Books © 2005

Library of Congress Cataloging-in-Publication data
is available on the Library of Congress website.
ISBN: 978-1-4048--6101-5 (library binding)
ISBN: 978-1-4048-6372-9 (paperback)

Art Director: KAY FRASER
Designer: EMILY HARRIS
Production Specialist: JANE KLENK

# TABLE OF CONTENTS

# CREEPY CRAWLERS:

## BUG AND INSECT JOKES

How is a fly swatter like a baseball bat?

They both hit flies.

What insects are found in clocks?

Ticks.

What do you say to
get rid of gnats?

Bug off!

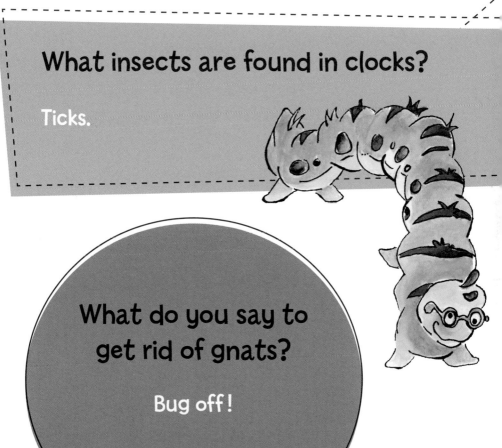

**Which bugs are the messiest?**

Litterbugs.

**When do bedbugs get married?**

In the spring.

**What's the name for a musical insect?**

A humbug.

## What happens to beekeepers?

They get hives.

## Which insects do well in school?

Spelling bees.

## What insect tells time?

Clockroaches.

# WHAT DOES AN OFFICIAL SAY TO START A FIREFLY RACE?

What do you get when you cross an insect with a rabbit?

Bugs bunny.

Which dance do insects prefer?

The jitterbug.

What did the grasshopper general say to his troops?

"Hop to!"

Why do spiders spin webs?

Because they can't knit.

Why do mosquitoes hum?

Because they don't know the words.

How do you revive a moth?

By using moth-to-moth resuscitation.

## What is a mosquito's favorite sport?

Skin diving.

## What's worse than a shark with a toothache?

A centipede with athlete's foot.

## What's the best transportation for infant insects?

A baby buggy.

Where do bees wait for a ride to school?

At the buzz stop.

Which insects do battle with knights?

Dragonflies.

How was the spider's secret plan discovered?

His phone was bugged.

# WHICH INSECTS ARE FAMOUS FOR BUILDING?

CARPENTER
ANTS.

Where do spiders get married?

At a webbing.

What do you call an ant that turns 100 years old?

An antique.

Where should you look for bucking broncos?

Among horseflies.

What do you call an ant that lives with your uncle?

Your anty.

What makes ticks so loyal?

When they make new friends, they really stick to them.

What was the largest prehistoric moth?

The mammoth.

What language do ticks speak?

Tick talk.

Which insect is famous for not being able to make up its mind?

The maybee.

Why did the baby firefly get a prize at school?

Because he was so bright for his age.

What wears spikes, has 18 legs, and catches flies?

A baseball team.

Which insects are known for their good manners?

Ladybugs.

How did the flower get rid of the bee?

She told him to buzz off.

What was the caterpillar's
New Year's resolution?

To turn over a new leaf.

What insect takes photographs?

A shutterbug.

How do bugs send messages?

By flea-mail.

Why was the young ant so confused?

Because all of his uncles were ants.

Where do insects go to buy and sell things?

The flea market.

What do bees call their sweethearts?

Honey.

Which insects got together to form a band?

The Beetles.

Which insects sleep the most?

Bedbugs.

What bees are the hardest to understand?

Mumblebees.

What insects do firefighters battle most often?

Fireflies.

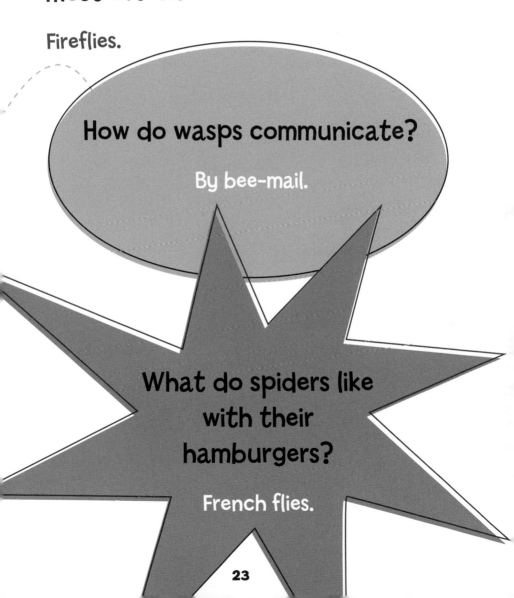

How do wasps communicate?

By bee-mail.

What do spiders like with their hamburgers?

French flies.

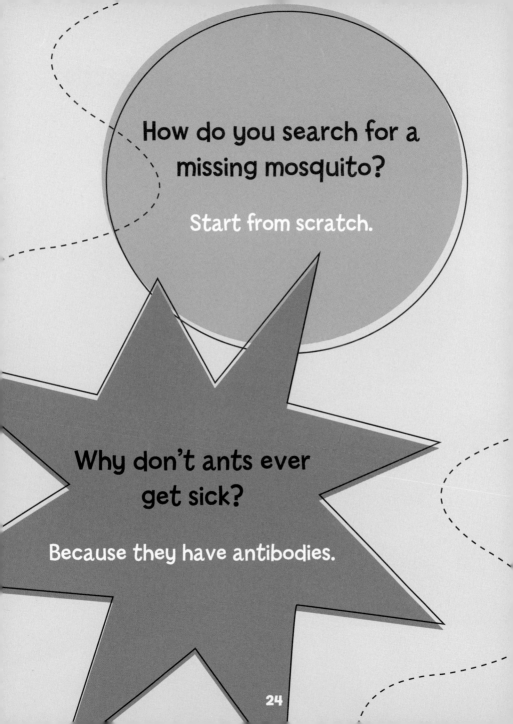

How do you search for a
missing mosquito?

Start from scratch.

Why don't ants ever
get sick?

Because they have antibodies.

What do you get when you eat caterpillars?

Butterflies in your stomach.

What kind of music do grasshoppers like?

Hip-hop.

How does a centipede count to 100?

On his feet.

# BEASTLY LAUGHS:

## CREATURE AND MONSTER JOKES

What's the Abominable Snowman's favorite game?

Freeze tag.

What is a monster's favorite part of a joke?

The punch line.

Why did the invisible man look in the mirror?

To see if he wasn't there.

**What happened when Dracula met the werewolf?**

They fought tooth and nail.

**What is Bigfoot's favorite cheese?**

Monsterella.

**Why wasn't Dr. Frankenstein ever lonely?**

Because he was so good at making new friends.

What did the director say
when he finished
his mummy movie?

That's a wrap.

Which side of a monster's mouth
has the sharpest teeth?

The inside.

Who's the center of attention
at a monster dance party?

The boogie man.

Why did King Kong climb to the top of the Empire State Building?

He was too big to use the elevator.

How did the giant snake find out that he wasn't poisonous?

He bit his tongue — and lived.

What is a monster's favorite sweet treat?

Ghoul Scout cookies.

What do sea monsters eat?

Fish and ships.

What do you call a monster who tells long, terrible stories?

A giant boar.

Why was the monster lonely on Halloween?

Because he missed his mummy.

When a monster puts his tooth under his pillow, who comes to get it?

The tooth scary.

What do you call Bigfoot in a bathtub?

Stuck.

What would you get if you crossed Godzilla with a teacher?

You'd get the kids to pay attention in class.

How do you contact an undersea monster?

You drop it a line.

Why didn't the giant snake use silverware?

Because he had a forked tongue.

How do you keep Godzilla from smelling?

Plug his nose.

Why was the monster pulling the rope?

Have you ever tried to push one?

What does Dr. Frankenstein's monster like for breakfast?

A big jolt of juice.

What time is it when a monster comes to dinner?

Time to leave.

What monster wears a mask and has a long gray trunk?

The Elephantom of the Opera.

Why are some monsters so quiet?

Because silence is ghoulden.

How do you make a green monster?

Cross a blue one with a yellow one.

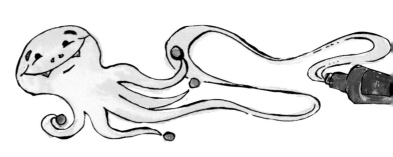

# WHAT DO YOU CALL ZOMBIES WITH LOTS OF KIDS?

MOMSTERS.

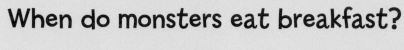

When do monsters eat breakfast?

Never before moaning.

What did the dragon say when he found the knight hiding under a rock?

You're toast.

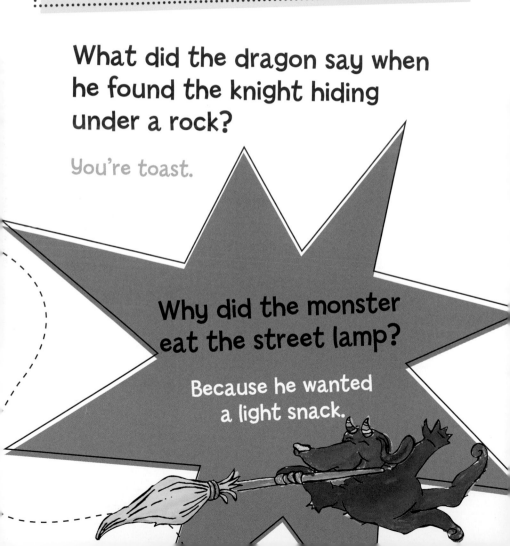

Why did the monster eat the street lamp?

Because he wanted a light snack.

What happened when the monster ran away with the circus?

The police made him bring it back.

Why didn't the monster eat the comedian?

Because he tasted funny.

Why did the mummy need a vacation?

He was coming unraveled.

**What has sharp claws and fangs and is green and slimy?**

I don't know, but it's crawling on your neck!

**What are giant alligator skins used for?**

To hold giant alligators together.

What position does a monster play in soccer?

Ghoulie.

What's Godzilla's favorite sport?

Dragon racing.

What's the one-eyed monster's favorite reference book?

The encyclopsedia.

MONSTER: I'VE BEEN SEEING SPOTS.

DR. FRANKENSTEIN: HAVE YOU SEEN A DOCTOR?

MONSTER: NO, JUST SPOTS.

Why did the monster eat people's brains?

He wanted food for thought.

What should you do if you find a monster in your bed?

Sleep in the guest room.

Where do monsters take their summer vacations?

On Lake Eerie.

**Where do monsters go to college?**
At gooniversities.

**Why do zombies make such good gardeners?**

Because they have green thumbs.

**Why wasn't there any food left after the monster party?**

Because everyone was a goblin.

What does the cyclops eat for dessert?

Eyes cream.

What dogs are the best pets for vampires?

Bloodhounds.

Why doesn't the vampire have many friends?

Because he's a pain in the neck.

What do you give
King Kong when he
sneezes?

Plenty of room!

What did the big hairy
monster do when he
lost a hand?

He went to the secondhand shop.

Why couldn't the mummy answer
the phone?

He was tied up.

What do you say to a
two-headed monster?

"Hello, hello!"

What kind of jewelry do ghosts
like to wear?

Tombstones.

What kind of music
do mummies like?

Wrap.

What do you get when you cross a ghost with a firecracker?

Bamboo.

What should you do if you meet a blue monster?

Try to cheer it up!

What's a vampire's favorite sport?

Batminton.

What movie do monsters watch again and again?

Scar Wars.

Why do monsters make such good hosts?

Because they like to have their friends for lunch.

How can you tell if there's a monster under your bed?

Your nose touches the ceiling.

How do you stop a werewolf from charging?

Take away his credit card.

What did the space monster say to the textbook?

Take me to your reader.

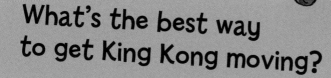

What's the best way to get King Kong moving?

A crane and a semitruck.

# WHY WAS THE ABOMINABLE SNOWMAN SO POPULAR?

# SPOOKY SILLIES:

## GHOST JOKES

What does a father ghost say when his son does something good?

"That's the spirit!"

How do you know that a school is haunted?

When it has school spirit.

What do ghosts put on their windows to keep out flies?

Screams.

How do you make a baby ghost stop crying?

Change his sheets.

What do you call a ghost's mistake?

A boo-boo.

What do you call a staircase in a haunted house?

A scarecase.

**What do ghosts like for breakfast?**

Booberry pancakes.

**Why was the skeleton afraid to cross the road?**

Because he didn't have the guts.

Why didn't the skeleton eat the cafeteria food?

Because he didn't have the stomach for it.

What do you call the ghost of a turkey?

A gobblin.

How do ghosts keep fit?

With a scaremaster.

**What do you call it when ghosts haunt a theater?**

Stage fright.

**What do sad ghosts say?**

Boo-hoo.

**What do they call a tired ghost after a long night's haunting?**

Dead on his feet.

What kind of birds do ghosts keep as pets?

Scarecrows.

What's a ghost's favorite Chinese food?

Fright rice.

Which room do ghosts always avoid?

The living room.

What do you call the ghost
of a horse?

A nightmare.

What do you call a zombie and
a ghost when they are dating?

Ghoulfriend and boofriend.

What ride do goblins love at
amusement parks?

The roller ghoster.

What do you get when a ghost sits in a tree?

Petrified wood.

What do you call a ghost who works as a fashion model?

A cover ghoul.

In what position do ghosts sleep?

Horrorzontal.

Where do ghosts take their kids when they go to work?

Dayscare centers.

Nurse: Doctor, there's a ghost waiting for an appointment.

Doctor: Tell him I can't see him.

What does a skeleton order for dinner?

Spareribs.

How do ghosts like their eggs for breakfast?

Terrifried.

Why was the ghost so lonely?

Because he had nobody.

What do you do at a ghost party?

Boogie.

What was the shy ghost's biggest problem?

He didn't believe in himself.

Why did the ghost stop hunting?

Because it was a dead-end job.

What do ghosts read
at a concert?

Sheet music.

What's a ghost's favorite
fairy tale?

Sleeping Booty.

What do ghosts like for breakfast?

Scream of wheat.

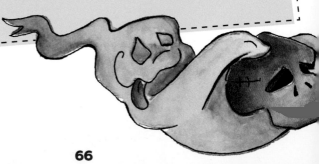

**Why don't ghosts ever tell lies?**

Because you can see right through them.

**What do you call the ghost of a chicken?**

A poultrygeist.

**What do ghosts put on their bagels?**

Scream cheese.

# WHAT DID THE COW DO WHEN SHE SAW A GHOST?

How do ghost parents dress their kids?

With pillowcases.

Why didn't the ghost go to the dance?

Because he had nobody to go with.

How can you tell when a ghost is sick?

He's white as a sheet.

How did the skeleton know
it was going to rain?

He felt it in his bones.

Where do ghosts go for treats?

The I-scream parlor.

What was the baby skeleton doing
with the textbooks?

He was boning up for a test.

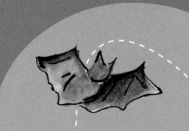

What did the sheet say to the ghost?

I've got you covered.

What steps should you take if a ghost is chasing you?

Big, fast ones.

What kind of pets do ghosts like best?

Scaredy cats.

Why don't skeletons play music in church?

Because they don't have any organs.

Why did one skeleton chase after the other?

Because he had a bone to pick.

How do ghosts shave?

With shaving scream.

# DINO RIB TICKLERS:

## DINOSAUR JOKES

Blah

Blah

Blah

What do you get when you cross
a Stegosaurus with a pig?

A porkyspine.

What sport does a T. rex
like to play?

Squash!

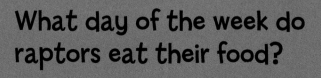

What day of the week do
raptors eat their food?

Chewsday.

Where was the Ultrasaurus when the sun set?

In the dark.

Why do museums display old dinosaur bones?

They can't afford new ones.

Where does a Triceratops sit?

On its Tricerabottom.

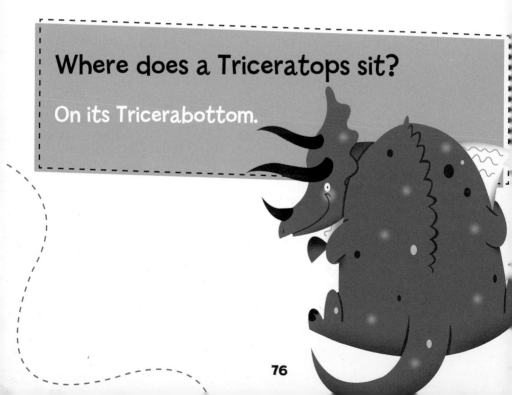

What makes more noise than a dinosaur?

Ten dinosaurs!

What do you call a dinosaur that talks and talks and talks?

A dinobore.

Why did the dinosaur cross the road?

It was the chicken's day off.

## How do you make a dinosaur float?

Take one dinosaur and add root beer and three scoops of ice cream.

## What toys do dinosaurs play with?

Triceratops.

Who is the fastest dinosaur?

A Prontosaurus.

What kind of music do dinosaurs make?

Rock.

What do you call a dinosaur who steps on a car?

Tyrannosaurus wrecks.

# HOW TO BE FUNNY

**KNOCK, KNOCK!**

The following tips will help you become rich, famous, and popular. Well, maybe not. However, they will help you tell a good joke.

## WHAT TO DO:

- Know the joke.
- Allow suspense to build, but don't drag it out too long.
- Make the punch line clear.
- Be confident, use emotion, and smile.

## WHAT NOT TO DO:

- Do not ask your friend over and over if they "get it."
- Do not speak in a different language than your audience.
- Do not tell the same joke every day.
- Do not keep saying, "This joke is so funny!"